Chickadee Winter

Dawn L. Watkins

Illustrated by
Gabriela Dellosso

JOURNEY
BOOKS
Greenville, South Carolina

Library of Congress Cataloging-in-Publication Data
Watkins, Dawn L.
    Chickadee Winter / Dawn L. Watkins ; illustrated by Gabriela Dellosso.
      p. cm.
    Summary: Jack does not think that he will enjoy the cold and snow of Christmas at his grandfather's house, so different from the hot climate he has known, but then he is delighted when Grandfather brings three chickadees inside and they become living decorations for the Christmas tree.
    ISBN 1-57924-273-1
    [1. Christmas Fiction. 2. Grandfathers Fiction. 3. Chickadees Fiction. 4. Christmas trees Fiction.] I. Dellosso, Gabriela, ill. II. Title.
PZ7.W268Ch   1999
[E]—dc21
                                       99-37151
                                          CIP

Chickadee Winter

Edited by Debbie L. Parker
Designed by Noelle Snyder and Duane A. Nichols

© 1999 Journey Books
Published by Bob Jones University Press
Greenville, South Carolina 29614

ISBN 1-57924-273-1

15 14 13 12 11 10 9 8 7 6 5 4 3 2 1

In memory of my grandparents,
Bruce and Louise
—DLW

To John,
for all his love and support
—GD

We got there just after the snow.

It was not like home at all.
It was too cold. Too quiet.
And I missed my friends.

New Mexico had been all the colors of warm:
Red, orange, yellow, gold-brown, cinnamon.
When the sun went down,
the whole world was bronze.

Nora, my sister, said, "Look! Clouds!"
and blew into the air—
air so cold it made my teeth ache.
Little cumulus clouds floated a moment,
then vanished.

1

And "Look! Feathers!" She pointed out
white, angled frost on windows.
I never knew that cold could paint on glass.
And I did not know of any bird
with such sharp white feathers.
Roadrunners have grey-brown tails
with only a few flecks of white.

But I saw here only
whiteness stretching out forever,
and at night I felt only keen-eyed stars
watching down and down.

"Listen!" Nora said, at the *scrunch-grunch,*
scrunch-grunch, scrunch-grunch of our boots.
"And listen," she said,
at the beady repeats of the chickadee.

> *Chick-a-dee-dee-dee.*
> *Chick-a-dee-dee-dee.*

I heard only the tall silence of the pines.

Nora ran to the feeder
to make the chickadees fly.
And up they flew in a thrum of wings
to the safety of the hemlocks.
"Chick-a-dee-dee-dee,"
they said down to us.

When Grandfather came out of the house,
the birds swirled toward him like a dust storm.
And it made him smile.

Somehow I understood why they did that.

4

We ate our suppers
with Grandfather and Grandmother.
There were never tacos or pizza.
We had beef stew and chicken and dumplings—
mounds of something like bread,
gooey on the outside
and dry as the desert inside.

I could only hope that the kitchen
in the farmhouse we bought
would get remodeled soon.

My mother said, "I grew up here."
My father said, "Come spring,
we'll plant a garden."
My sister said, "How high will the snow get?"
I said nothing.
If you don't have anything good to say,
don't say anything at all—that's the rule.

The only good thing was Grandfather.

He was a winter man.

His hair was white and smooth like a drift;

his eyes were ice blue like a Christmas sky.

He was always quiet,

like the pines in the snow.

8

I crunched behind him to the barn.
Scruncha-grunch. Scruncha-grunch.
I shadowed him when he milked the cows,
in the stillness of the barn,
the cows snuffling
through their hay-dinners.

I helped him carry wood
and build fires in the fireplace.
I supposed that I would need to know
how to build a fire,
because evenings can get chilly in the West.

9

I stomped in his prints to the tops of hills.
I stood beside him when he looked
at next summer's trees.
He never asked me any questions.
He never told me how much better
this was than New Mexico.

Every morning and night,
he fed the chickadees.
They flicked around him.

Chick-a-dee-dee-dee.
Chick-a-dee-dee-dee.

They darted at his cap
and the scoop he carried.

They sat on his hat.
They hung under the bill
and looked him in the eye.
They rode on the button.
They flew behind him to the feeder.

11

Sometimes they came to the window
to look for him.
They flicked by, clamoring for attention.
Sometimes they even clicked the panes
with their beaks.
"Better go see what they want," he would say.

Nora asked him, "Why do they let you
come up to them,
but they fly away from me?"
He finished filling the feeders
and put the scoop away before he answered.

"They are used to me," he said.
"They just need a little more time;
they'll get used to you.
Things take some getting used to."

Then he looked at me.
I couldn't tell whether he wanted to see
what I thought of Nora's question,
or whether he wanted to know something else.

It snowed again just before Christmas.
The snow got almost as high as Nora.
"Oh," she said, "what a wonderful
Christmas this will be."
I went to see if I had any mail
from New Mexico,
but I didn't.

Our grandparents' Christmas tree was up
in the living room with nothing on it yet.

It was a blue spruce our grandfather had cut
from the edge of his woods.
It looked like a green *A*.

15

"Grandma wants us to make it be
Christmas in here," Nora said.
"You do it," I said.
"Come on, Jack," she said.
"Grandma has ribbons,
and real bells, and even these little glass icicles."
"No," I said. I wondered whether
Mom had brought the strings
of red pepper lights from home.

Nora looked at our grandfather
the way she looks at Dad
when she wants money.
But Grandfather only smiled a little smile at her,
and went on reading the paper.

The next day, just before supper,
Grandfather came in from feeding the birds.
He didn't stop to hang up his cap and coat.
He didn't stomp off the snow on the mat.

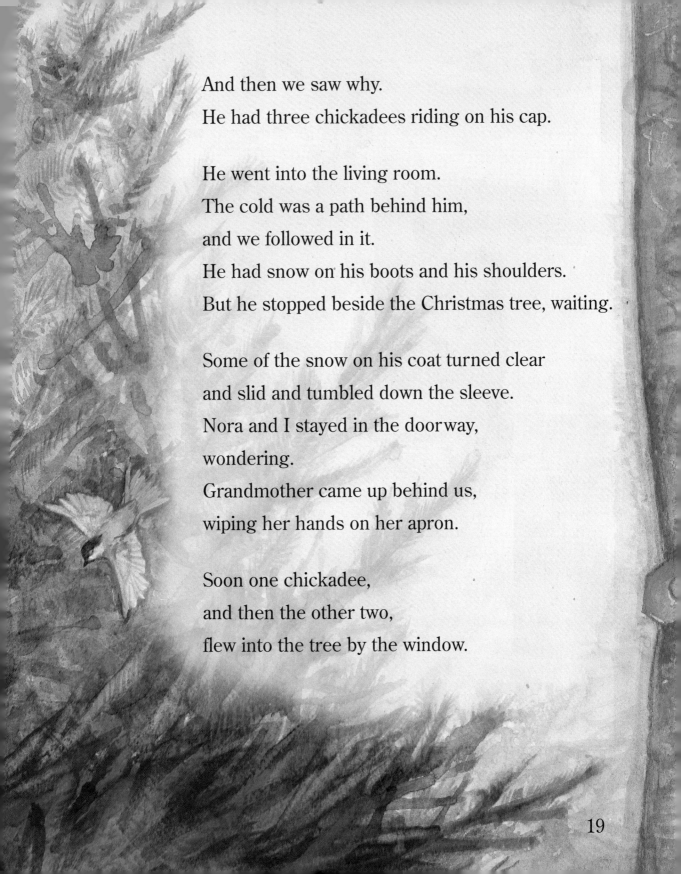

And then we saw why.

He had three chickadees riding on his cap.

He went into the living room.

The cold was a path behind him,

and we followed in it.

He had snow on his boots and his shoulders.

But he stopped beside the Christmas tree, waiting.

Some of the snow on his coat turned clear

and slid and tumbled down the sleeve.

Nora and I stayed in the doorway,

wondering.

Grandmother came up behind us,

wiping her hands on her apron.

Soon one chickadee,

and then the other two,

flew into the tree by the window.

Still Grandfather stood there, waiting.
Then, after a long time—

    Chick-a-dee-dee-dee.
    Chick-a-dee-dee-dee.

The little birds flitted to different branches.
They sang and sang from the blue spruce tree,
as though they had come home from far away.

My grandmother opened her mouth.
She was going to say something
about the furniture
and what birds might do to it, I thought.
But she never did.

We just stood there and looked at the only tree
Grandfather had ever decorated.
A Christmas tree with live decorations
that moved and sang and looked at us.
The best Christmas tree anyone had ever seen.

When Grandfather opened his hand,
there was seed in it.
He put some on his cap.
The chickadees came to him,
like always,
like bits of metal to a magnet.

They fluttered around him,
and took their places
and the seeds.

And they all went out again
into the snow and the cold,
the little birds and Grandfather.

More birds flew around him at the red feeder.
They chick-a-deed him.
They made me laugh.
They looked like little planes swooping a tower.

That night, after supper and milking,
Nora and I looked out the kitchen window.
The lights from inside pushed the dark
a little way out from the house.

My sister said, "Look,"
and pointed to the icy branches
clicking on the windowpane.
"Clear Popsicles."

She made me laugh too.
She took my hands and danced around.
"Now," she said, "let's do the tree. Please?"

Grandfather came in from the barn.

He snapped his cap against his knee

and hung it by the door.

"Look," I said to him and pointed at my sister.

Still fluttering around.

"She's a chickadee."

25

He smiled his little smile.

"Better see what she wants," he said.

So Nora and I went to decorate.

We hung up the bells and the glass icicles.

And Nora strung the ribbons

down the branches.

We both stood back to look.

"It's nice," she said.

"But not as nice

as with Grandpa's decorations."

Nothing would ever be that good.

I smiled a smile like Grandfather's.

"No," I said, "but we'll get used to it."

Books written by Dawn L. Watkins

Medallion
Jenny Wren
The Cranky Blue Crab
A King for Brass Cobweb
Very Like a Star
Wait and See
Zoli's Legacy Book I: Inheritance
Zoli's Legacy Book II: Bequest
Pocket Change
Pulling Together
The Spelling Window
Once in Blueberry Dell
Nantucket Cats
Chickadee Winter

Books illustrated by Gabriela Dellosso

Pelts and Promises
Trouble at Silver Pines Inn
Anne of Green Gables (Macmillan)
Cave People (Grosset & Dunlap)
Indian School (Harper Collins)
Chickadee Winter